PONG

PIG

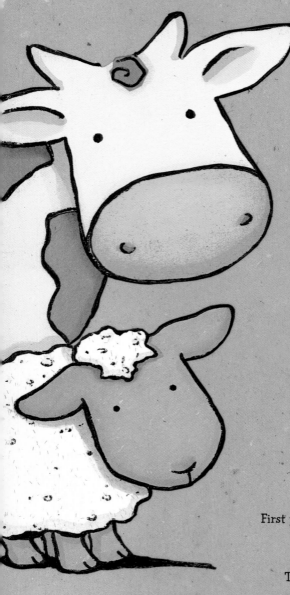

For Charlotte S
CJC

Simon and Schuster
First published in Great Britain in 2008 by Simon and Schuster UK Ltd
Africa House, 64-78 Kingsway, London, WC2B 6AH
A CBS Company

A CIP catalogue record for this book is available from
the British Library upon request

ISBN: 978 1 84738 207 8 (HB)
ISBN: 978 1 84738 208 5 (PB)

Printed in China

1 3 5 7 9 10 8 6 4 2

Caroline Jayne Church

PING PONG PIG

SIMON AND SCHUSTER
London New York Sydney

Apple Tree Farm was a very busy place.
Every day the animals would rush this way
and that doing their daily chores.

All the animals worked very hard indeed.
All, that is, except one . . .

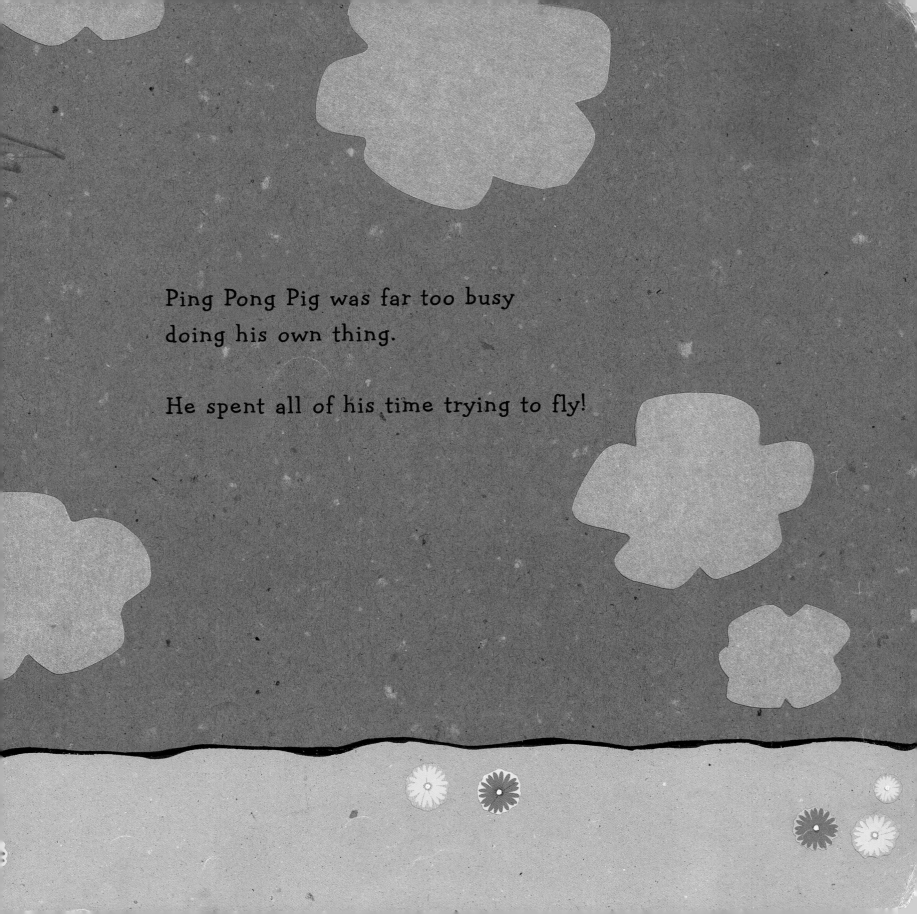

Ping Pong Pig was far too busy
doing his own thing.

He spent all of his time trying to fly!

He leapt from fences
and logs . . .

. . . wheelbarrows and
barrels, trying to jump
higher and higher.

"One day I will be able to fly,"
he told the other animals.

"Pigs can't fly, Ping Pong,"
they sighed.

But Ping Pong never stopped jumping and leaping.

He managed to ruin the apples . . .

spoil the new paint on the barn . . .

free the bees . . .

and knock over all the hay!

The animals decided that something had to be done.
They gathered together for a meeting in the barn.

Ping Pong wondered what was going on.
The animals stayed in the barn all morning.
They were obviously very busy.

At last, the barn doors swung open
and the animals came out.
Ping Pong looked on in amazement.

"We've made you this trampoline,"
they said. "Now take it to a quiet corner
of the field and let us get on with our work."

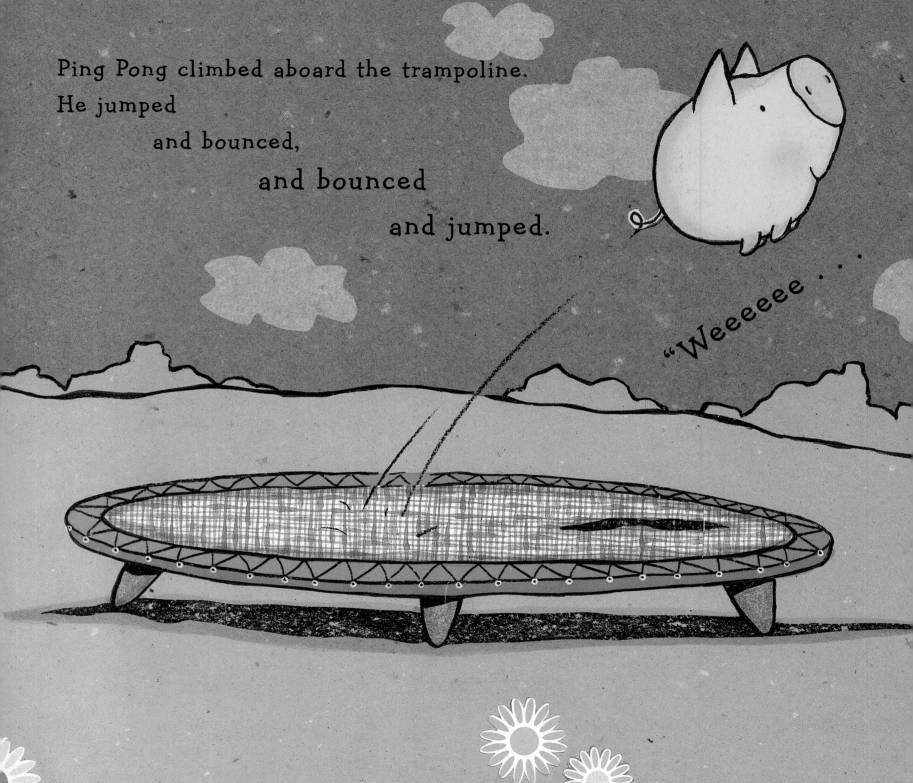

Ping Pong climbed aboard the trampoline.
He jumped
   and bounced,
      and bounced
         and jumped.

"Weeeeee . . . .

can fly!" he squealed.

"But pigs can't fly, Ping Pong," the animals
sighed as they went to get on with their work.

Ping Pong Pig was having the best time EVER!

But then he stopped to have a little think.
"It was so kind of my friends to make me this present.
Perhaps I should help out a little more as a way of
saying, 'thank you'?" So he decided to put his
trampoline to better use.

He picked the apples . . .

caught the bees . . .

repainted the barn . . .

and carefully stacked all the hay.

Much to his surprise, Ping Pong
rather enjoyed helping out and
his friends were delighted.

"No more trouble from Ping Pong Pig!"
they all said . . .

...until something caught their eye.

High at the top of the old apple tree,
they noticed something rustling.

It was Ping Pong Pig!

"Look!" shouted Ping Pong,
as he leapt from the branches,

"Pigs CAN fly!"

"No, Ping Pong!"
cried the animals.

But it was too late.

SPLASH!

Ping Pong landed in the middle of the pond.
"Wow, fish can fly too!" he giggled.